iUniverse books may be ordered through booksellers or by contacting:

iUniverse
1663 Liberty Drive
Bloomington, IN 47403
www.iuniverse.com
1-800-Authors (1-800-288-4677)

Because of the dynamic nature of the Internet, any web addresses or links contained in this book may have changed since publication and may no longer be valid. The views expressed in this work are solely those of the author and do not necessarily reflect the views of the publisher, and the publisher hereby disclaims any responsibility for them.

Any people depicted in stock imagery provided by Getty Images are models, and such images are being used for illustrative purposes only.
Certain stock imagery © Getty Images.

ISBN: 978-1-5320-6400-5 (sc)
ISBN: 978-1-5320-6402-9 (hc)
ISBN: 978-1-5320-6401-2 (e)

Library of Congress Control Number: 2019901443

Print information available on the last page.

iUniverse rev. date: 02/07/2019

BLAZE

THE
DRAGON

The Adventures of Ra-me,
The Traveling Troubadour-Book 2

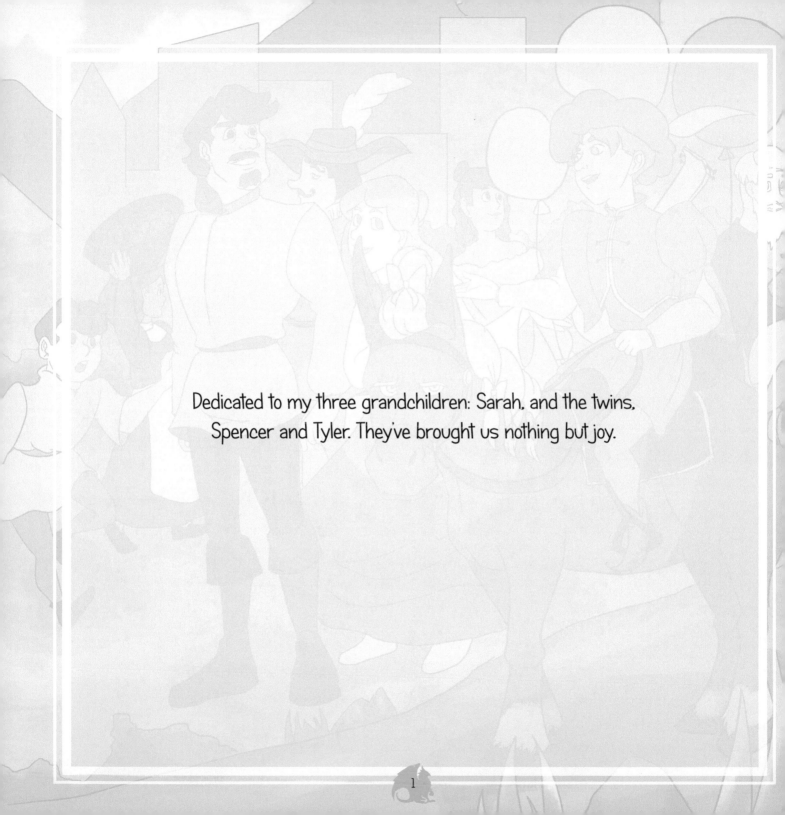

Dedicated to my three grandchildren: Sarah, and the twins, Spencer and Tyler. They've brought us nothing but joy.

Blaze the Dragon

"You say it's my turn, Falstaff? O. K., I'll begin."

Once upon a time... Oh, I can't say once upon a time, because I think it happened to Nessie of the Loch Ness.

Falstaff and I are boon companions, but for those of you staying in this inn tonight who don't know me, my name is Ra-me—you know as in do-re-mi-fa-so-la-ti-do. I'm a freelance minstrel and a traveling troubadour. The things that've happened to me!

"Ah, I know, Falstaff, I'm wandering from my story. Yes, it's a new one. Of course, it's true; I know that skeptical look of yours."

Well, after my successful gig at Parkingham Castle, I had an invitation to play at Dragon Village. Blaze, the Dragon, was to be twelve-years-old, and his parents were giving him a coming-of-age birthday party which was why all his dragon aunts, uncles, and cousins would be there. At the age of twelve, his dragon training would begin. He'd learn to roar until the ground shook, throw flames, make his eyes glow red, protect a castle, and battle a knight if it became necessary.

"I can tell you, Falstaff, just holding the invitation in my hand was scary. I didn't know if it would be safe to go. And, I didn't think it would be smart to say 'no' to a dragon named Inferno. But I knew I had to accept this invitation to play at the party."

I polished my harp, restrung my lute, packed my silken blouses and breeches. I tied colorful balloons to Roscoe's saddle, making him look as festive as possible. On my journey, I passed the time to good advantage. I wrote poems to delight a young boy and set them to music as I rode. I tried to forget that he was indeed a dragon.

In my pocket was a permission slip for safe passage through Dragon Village. It read:

> RA-ME, TROUBADOUR AND SINGER OF ALL SONGS, HEREBY HAS PERMISSION TO TRAVEL, UNHARMED, TO DRAGON VILLAGE. HE WILL ALSO BE ALLOWED TO LEAVE SAFELY. HE WILL ENTERTAIN AT THE COMING-OF-AGE BIRTHDAY PARTY. HE WILL BE UNHARMED WHILE THERE. DRAGONS DO NOT EAT TROUBADOURS. SOMETIMES THEY HAVE SOUR NOTES.
>
> HOWEVER, IT MIGHT BE BEST FOR HIS MULE TO BE TIED OUTSIDE THE BOUNDARIES OF DRAGON TERRITORY.
>
> TRUTHFULLY YOURS,
>
> INFERNO, HEAD DRAGON
> FATHER OF BLAZE

The note kept saying that I'd be safe. I hoped it was not just a trick to get me there.

I left Roscoe tethered near a running stream. Grass grew up to his withers, so he was well hidden. He was grazing happily when I started toward the village on foot.

The path that led to the main cave was well-traveled and marked with dragon footprints. The note in my pocket didn't seem like enough protection!

When I finally arrived, this giant dragon emerged from a large cave, his shadow blocking out the sun.

"Ah, Ra-me, glad you found us," he roared.

"Now, Falstaff, you know I like a bag of gold as well as the next fella, but I'm not greedy. I was shaking in my boots."

"We've had an accident," he continued to roar. "Blaze fell into the creek! When a young dragon falls into the water and goes completely under, he sometimes loses his fire. I'm afraid Blaze's flame has been put out by the water. I am distraught. But since everyone is here, the coming-of-age party must go on."

I told him how sorry I was. Now, maybe I could go home.

"But are you Ra-me, the much-lauded troubadour?" He growled at me.

I nodded yes.

He continued, "Then you are just in time. If all of the entertainment we have planned doesn't light his fire, then you can do something to get his blaze back."

I was speechless. I felt my knees buckling from under me. I straightened quickly. I didn't want Inferno to know how afraid I was. But I was no fire-bug!

"Oh, you're tired. I know you've had a long journey," said Inferno. "I'll take you to the guest cave. Tomorrow the party will begin, and it may be enough to re-light Blaze's fire."

I followed Inferno to the smallest cave on the outskirts of the village. The cave's interior did nothing to put my fears to rest. Family pictures were painted on the cave walls in red. Probably blood! Scenes showed dragons at war with knights. The dragons always looked like the winners with their enormous feet on top of the flapping knights. In one story, the dragon had slain St. George! Flames shot out of every mouth and nostril.

I'd seen bones on the floor, and I thought I could feel them sticking my back coming up through the blanket. I wouldn't get any sleep that night!

The sun rose brightly on what would probably be my last day on earth. I could hear the dragon families at breakfast. Strong jaws were crunching bones. The table was loaded with haunches of venison, slabs of ribs, racks of lamb, whole roasted pigs with apples in their mouths. A tank of fish. One table was heaped with fruits and vegetables for the vegan family that ate no meat.

I took a turnip and went to my bandstand to start the music. It didn't really matter what song I played. The dragons were so loud and boisterous that I was just a muffled background. But play I did! Just as loudly as I could. It helped me keep my mind off of my future.

From my high seat, I could see Blaze sitting at the end of the birthday table. His parents were sitting on either side of him, but his head was drooping nearly into his plate.

Inferno stood and announced that it was time for everyone to get ready for the festivities to begin. A rousing cheer went up.

My ears rang. I would certainly have a headache when I left Dragon Village. If, I would be allowed to go!

All the dragons that were going to perform ran to their caves to get into their costumes.

The other dragons had left the tables and had made a circle, leaving an entrance to a large arena where the performers would show off their talents.

Suddenly, it became quiet. All eyes were on a figure emerging from his cave.

WOW! I was impressed. I stared, but a frown from Inferno told me that I should be playing.

Softly, I began to pluck the strings of my lute, playing a haunting melody of China Town.

There, entering the ring, was the most colorful creature that I'd ever seen. He was the parade dragon from China. The sun glittered off of his costume until I had to pull my hat down to shade my eyes. He glowed in his shimmering fuchsia and chartreuse green silks. His eyes were round, green and as shiny as glass balls on a Christmas Tree. Large teeth were few, but they came to dangerous-looking points. His snake-like neck was long and flexible, allowing his head to go slowly from side to side. Golden horns stuck up on each side of his head. Golden spikes traveled down his back and ended like a whip on the end of his tail.

Cheers, whistles, and clapping followed him all the way into the center of the ring. The two smaller dragons with him stood in the middle of the arena. They stooped down and anchored sticks that looked like candles in a semi-circle around the arena. The small dragons then left the ring.

Everyone was quiet again. Something was going to happen.

Slowly, the dragon moved his head around the circle of the crowd. When he was sure that he had everyone's attention, he turned his eyes to the sticks in the ground around him. With perfect aim, he blew his flame to each rod, and the candles caught fire.

Now, I knew. The sticks were fireworks. One, two, and more, they exploded around him and burst into the sky. Even in the daylight, their multi-colored brilliance outshone the sun. Noise and smoke filled the arena.

My music got louder as the Chinese Dragon danced and writhed within his circle of fire. I loved this! My music became part of the scene below me. I might not leave Dragon Village alive, but I was enjoying myself now.

The Chinese Dragon took his bows and slowly left the arena to go back into his cave.

I looked over at Blaze the Dragon. I was sure that I would see little flames from his mouth. But, alas, not even a spark. But he was smiling his toothy grin.

After all that excitement, there was an intermission. The dragons all grabbed goblets, drinking thirstily. I tried not to think about what was in the cups.

All the dragons were seated again, waiting for the next act. When I saw the costumes on this set of dragons, I changed the music to Mexican melodies. My rhythm changed, and the clapping from the crowd added the sound of maracas. Their nails clicking on the rocks sounded like castanets. Together, we sure had a rocking sound going. Loved it!

Wide-brimmed sombreros shaded their faces; gaily woven serapes hung around their necks. I did riffs on my lute, keeping in rhythm with the dancers' steps, and we played and played. Everyone was shouting "ole."

I must confess that I got caught up in the moment. The Spanish dancers' steps weren't graceful, and their movements weren't very flowing. When the dance was finished, the dancers lumbered out of the arena.

The crowd rose to their feet in a frenzy of delight.

I looked again at Blaze the Dragon.

His eyes were bright and shiny, but the little puffs forced from his mouth were only small wisps of invisible air.

Two more dragons came to the center stage, carrying what looked like framework for a hangman's noose. I might be in trouble!

The crowd again was quiet, waiting.

After that, came two Mexican dragons carrying a piñata, fashioned like a donkey, which they hung from the frame.

The two dragons began to dance around the piñata. Lifting their tails, they swung at the target. Again, and again, they flipped their tails at the donkey. When they finished the dance, they motioned for all the kiddie dragons to come and swing their tails at the piñata. It broke open, and dragon treats scattered all over the ground.

From the same cave, a dragon wearing a bull's head mask ran to the center of the arena. He was followed by a dragon wearing a toreador's cape. The bull jumped and twisted in the air as the toreador jabbed a make-believe sword at him. Now everyone was shouting, "*el Toro*! But the bullfighter did one final jab, and the bull fell.

"Dust and dragon breath filled the air! Falstaff, I could hardly breathe."

Lunchtime brought more bone-crunching from the dragon's table, and I went back to my guest cave to eat my two apples. I washed off all the dragon dust and drank water to clear my throat. If this entertainment didn't give Blaze the Dragon his fire back, I'd better have a powerful song.

Lunch was over, and I climbed back up onto my platform. I'd worked on my music and was ready to play again. The arena had been swept clean, and we were waiting for the next act. I played merry tunes. I hadn't been given a playlist, so I didn't know what to expect.

The next act was beginning. Props were carried into the center of the arena: A tall black box, a long table and a smaller table with a cloth-covered object on it. I accompanied all this with some eerie melodies and frightening words.

Then, the actor rushed out. He was a medium-sized dragon all covered with green scales. On his black cape was the name 'Puff'. I guessed he was going to do magic.

And, I was right. He made a lady dragon disappear inside the tall black box. With a few abracadabras, he brought her back. Everyone cheered. That same lady dragon then lay on the table.

14

"Now, Falstaff, this was really a trick. He made that large lady rise in the air, nothing between her and the table. I looked and looked, but I couldn't even see a wire, a rope, anything. I heard later he must've learned that trick when he lived by the sea."

I looked again at Blaze the Dragon. His eyes got huge at this trick, but not a flicker of a flame.

For Puff's last act, he removed his hat, and white pigeons flew out and over the crowd. They were quickly snatched from the air. Next, he pulled three white rabbits out of his hat and juggled them above his head. One by one as they came down, he swallowed each of them. I didn't think these rabbits would appear again. He twirled his black cape and bowed. I was sure this was the end of the magician's act. Then, in a big billow of dark smoke, he disappeared.

The crowd went wild. They loved this magic dragon.

Inferno stood in front of the crowd and raised his paws. It got quiet.

"We have one more treat for you. I think I hear it coming!"

On the horizon, we all could see something. It was big! It was black! Its wings sounded like a mighty windstorm. And, it was coming straight toward us all. It flew in and landed on my bandstand. I cowered down in terror.

"Fear not, Troubadour!" The giant creature screeched. "I'm here to help Blaze celebrate his coming-of-age birthday."

He pulled a feather from his wing and tossed it toward Blaze. It soared and did loop-d-loops before it came to rest in front of the bedazzled Blaze.

"What a privilege! Our great, grand-master Griffin has honored Blaze with a visit."

It was a griffin! I had only heard of them. Never wanted to see one. But he was magnificent. Strong back legs and hips of a lion, regal head of an eagle. His lion's roar ended with the scream of an eagle.

I put my hand into my pocket to assure myself that my safe-attendance note was still there. It was wrinkled and sweaty after all this time, but I had it.

If the crowd had been loud before, it now sent roars that bounced from mountain top to mountain top and back again. My bandstand shook.

He bowed to all. Then, the big dragon-bird encircled the arena twice and soared back into the air. We all watched as he disappeared.

"Maybe the griffin's feather will cure Blaze," Inferno said. "Griffins' feathers have some healing powers."

Blaze's mother brought out a birthday cake. On it were twelve large candles.

"Everyone, stand back," said Inferno. "Give Blaze room."

He picked up the feather from the Griffin. Carefully, he waved it over Blaze's head and tickled his nose until he sneezed.

"Now, Blaze, light your candles," his father said.

Blaze bent forward, puckered his lips and blew. Nothing. He blew again. Not even a tiny puff of smoke.

A moan went up from the crowd.

"Okay, Ra-me, master troubadour, singer of songs. Blaze must have his fire back. He'll be the mighty leader after I'm gone. Perform something that will bring back Blaze's spirit," commanded Inferno.

"Now, Falstaff, I didn't sign up for this. I just came to sing and play."

It was so quiet that I could hear my knees knock. Everyone looked at me and waited. Inferno was frowning.

Okay. This was it. I had to try to find some magic of my own.

My music started slowly and softly. I told how, as an unhatched egg, his mother polished him every day. She kept him turned to the sun. The day the egg cracked, and he bounced out, his parents laughed and danced.

As he grew, everyone loved Blaze and knew he would become a mighty leader like his father. But one day there was an accident. He tumbled into a deep hole of water, and his head went under! He was thoroughly soaked, and his fire went out.

I had the crowd's attention, and they were listening to my every word. So, I sang louder.

"We love Blaze," I sang. "We all want to help him."

Smoke rings shaped like hearts began to come from the dragons' mouths and circled around Blaze.

"Ooh," the crowd crooned.

The smoke rings began to turn red. Valentine hearts floated all around. Now all the air around Blaze was becoming rosy.

"Aah," the crowd crooned more loudly.

The air became hot. I could see drops of sweat beading on Blaze's snout.

Suddenly, Blaze stood up directly in front of his birthday cake.

He puffed, puffed again. A finger-like flame shot out of his mouth and lit the first candle. Then he puffed eleven more times, and all the candles burst into flame.

"Thank you, Ra-me!" shouted Blaze.

Quickly, I sang a little chorus, "It takes love to light a fire, it takes love to light a fire...It's our gift to share, to show our friends we care..." I don't remember the rest of the words. Maybe I will later.

What a celebration! Everyone was happy. And very loud.

"Well, Falstaff, I thought this would be a good time for me to make my getaway. So, I turned and started down the road."

"Wait, troubadour!" growled Inferno. Thunderous footsteps followed me.

I stopped. I knew I could never outrun him.

"We want to thank you," he said. "Wear this in your hat." He handed me their most prized possession—the feather from the Griffin. You will always be welcomed in Dragon Village as long as you are wearing this feather." Then he added, "But you still better leave your mule outside our territory."

"And we want you to have this little token of thanks, too." He handed me a bag of precious, shining jewels.

"Th-th-thank you," I stuttered.

I was really going to get to leave Dragon Village, unharmed.

When I was out of their sight, I ran as fast as I could to where I had left Roscoe. He was glad to see me, and we were both delighted to be going home.

Printed in the United States
By Bookmasters